tate publishing
CHILDREN'S DIVISION

a Wheel Rainbow

Addie Mercer Zannes
and
Bonnie Kyllo Mercer

Published by Tate Publishing & Enterprises, LLC
127 E. Trade Center Terrace | Mustang, Oklahoma 73064 USA
1.888.361.9473 | www.tatepublishing.com

Tate Publishing is committed to excellence in the publishing industry. The company reflects the philosophy established by the founders, based on Psalm 68:11,
"The Lord gave the word and great was the company of those who published it."

Book design copyright © 2015 by Tate Publishing, LLC. All rights reserved.
Cover and interior design by Cecille Kaye Gumadan
Illustrations by Cleoward Sy

Published in the United States of America
ISBN: 978-1-63449-823-4
Juvenile Fiction / General
14.11.05

This book is for all the moms and dads who hear their preschoolers say, "Read it again, again, and again."

Mommy, do you know what this is? It's a rainbow with wheels.

If I had a rainbow with wheels, I'd push it into my room and slide down it onto my bed.

I'd play "London Bridge" with my rainbow.

I'd like to go swimming with my rainbow.

I'd let my brother play with my rainbow too.

I can play on the clouds if I have a rainbow.

My rainbow will help me
pick apples.

I would win a coasting race
with my rainbow.

In the winter, I can slide down a snowy hill.

If it rained a lot, I would be safe in my rainbow boat.

My rainbow is my
best friend.

One day, the clouds came to take my rainbow away.

But before they could get it,
I wished it to be very, very
small and put it in my mouth.

Now, every day I can share
my wheel rainbow smile!

e|LIVE

listen|imagine|view|experience

AUDIO BOOK DOWNLOAD INCLUDED WITH THIS BOOK!

In your hands you hold a complete digital entertainment package. In addition to the paper version, you receive a free download of the audio version of this book. Simply use the code listed below when visiting our website. Once downloaded to your computer, you can listen to the book through your computer's speakers, burn it to an audio CD or save the file to your portable music device (such as Apple's popular iPod) and listen on the go!

How to get your free audio book digital download:

1. Visit www.tatepublishing.com and click on the e|LIVE logo on the home page.
2. Enter the following coupon code:
   6305-71ee-8e61-fb9e-faa9-786a-9de2-7353
3. Download the audio book from your e|LIVE digital locker and begin enjoying your new digital entertainment package today!